SID FLEISCHMAN
The Scarebird

PICTURES BY
PETER SIS

A Mulberry Paperback Book, New York

For Zachary
—S. F.

For Susan
—P. S.

Oil paints were used for
the full-color art.
The text type is Novarese.

Text copyright © 1987
by Sid Fleischman, Inc.
Illustrations copyright © 1988
by Peter Sis

Printed in the
United States of America

First Mulberry Edition, 1994.
10 9 8 7 6 5 4 3 2 1

Library of Congress
Cataloging-in-Publication Data

Fleischman, Sid, 1920–
The scarebird / Sid Fleischman ;
pictures by Peter Sis.
p.   cm.
Summary: A lonely, old farmer
realizes the value of human
friendship when a young man
comes to help him and his
scarecrow with their farm.
ISBN 0-688-13105-0
[1. Friendship–Fiction.
2. Scarecrows–Fiction.
3. Farm life–Fiction.]
I. Sis, Peter, ill. II. Title.
PZ7.F5992Sc   1994
[E]–dc20   93-11726   CIP   AC

One time a lonely old farmer jammed some old clothes
full of straw and put up a scarecrow.
But the scarecrow had no head.
"Just keep the cuss-hollering birds out of the corn patch,"
said the farmer. "You don't need a head for that."
It was true. Crows and blackbirds circled the long-armed,
long-legged scarecrow and kept at a safe distance.

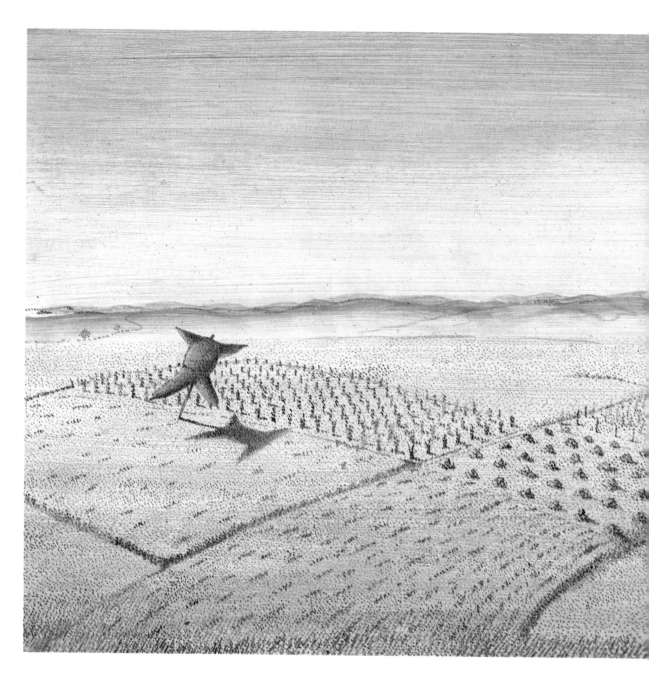

But as the first days of spring passed, the farmer—called Lonesome John by the folks in town—grew uneasy. Everytime he looked up from his chores, there stood that headless scarecrow.
And after supper, when he sat on the porch and played his nickle-plated harmonica, there against the fading sun stood the headless scarecrow.

"If that's not the most fearsome sight I ever saw, it'll do,"
said Lonesome John in a loud voice. With his family gone
and his old dog Sallyblue buried in the pasture, he had
no one left to talk to but himself.
"That scarebird's enough to give a man the cold creeps."

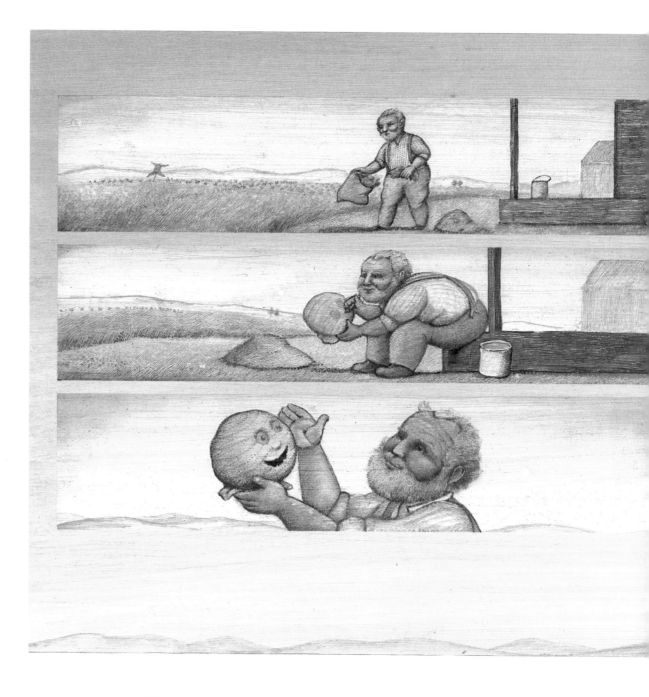

The next morning Lonesome John hunted up an old
pillowcase and stuffed it with straw. He used house
paint to dab on a pair of yellow eyes. A hole in the
pillowcase would do for a mouth.

He sauntered to the corn patch and fixed the head
to the neck of the scarecrow.
"Does that face suit you, Scarebird? You look like
sunshine on stilts with them yeller-paint eyes!
Well, make yourself at home."

The next day, when Lonesome John went out to start up
his tractor, he gave a wave. "Mornin', Scarebird! I slept
like a pine log. How about you!"

And in the evenings, when he sat on the front porch
playing his nickle-plated harmonica, he felt almost
as if the scarecrow could hear every note.
"See you tomorrow, Scarebird!" he'd call out when
he went in to bed.

Lonesome John was sleeping like a pine log when he was awakened by wind banging the barn door. He'd heard wind before, and went back to sleep. At daybreak, with the wind now howling and shrieking in his ears, he jumped out of bed.

The scarebird!

He looked out the window. There stood the scarecrow, face to the wind, holding his ground. Lonesome John grinned.

"I figured you were a goner, Scarebird!"

But when he squinted his eyes, he saw the wind was plucking straw from the scarecrow's cuffs and carrying off its hands and feet.

Lonesome John rushed outside with a pair of shoes and
work gloves, and his pockets full of fresh straw. Within
minutes he had replaced the straw in the cuffs, put the
gloves on, and laced the shoes up tight.

"You're good as new, Scarebird, and a little better." And
then he added, "Ain't you all dressed up! Those are my
town shoes, but I hardly go to town anymore so you're
welcome to them."

The wind whisked itself away. The days turned hot. Before
long the sun was rising like a blowtorch at full blast.
"Mornin', Scarebird. Looks like another scorcher today."
Every time Lonesome John glanced up from his farm chores,
there stood the scarecrow bareheaded under the flaming
sun. He remembered how ol' Sallyblue used to head
for the shade under the house on summer days like this.

"Scarebird, you need a hat," he called.
He picked out his wide-brimmed straw hat, his town hat,
and set it on the scarecrow's head. He pulled the brim
low over the sunflower yellow eyes.
"That's my bettermost hat, but you're welcome to it."

The hot spell passed, the evenings cooled off, and after
supper Lonesome John sat on the porch playing old
tunes on his nickle-plated harmonica.
"See you tomorrow, Scarebird."
But dark clouds tumbled in during the night, and when
Lonesome John awoke he could smell rain. And he heard
the windows chattering like baby rattles.
"It's going to rain blue thunderbolts!"

He rushed outside with his yellow slicker, pulled the
arms of the scarecrow through the sleeves, and threw the
hood over the wide-brimmed hat. When he had the rain
gear buttoned, he looked up at the swollen clouds.
"Yes sir, blue thunderbolts. Won't do to have you get
soaked through and mold up, will it?"

The earth was drying out when Lonesome John hunted up his old checkerboard. He set an apple box in front of the scarecrow and opened the board.

"How about a game of checkers? I ain't played since the boys left home, so I'll be a mite rusty. You go first."

Lonesome John moved a checker for the scarecrow and then one for himself. Before long the game was far along and Lonesome John was in deep concentration.

"Your move, Scarebird."

Lonesome John hardly noticed the time pass. "King me,
Scarebird! I ain't licked yet!"
Then a shadow fell across the checkerboard.
He looked up and saw a young man in worn jeans standing
there, barefooted and bareheaded.
"Howdy, sir. Folks in town said you might need a hired hand."
"I get along by myself," answered Lonesome John.
"Yes, sir."

Lonesome John wanted to get back to the checker game, but the
stranger looked foot-weary and hardly more than sixteen or so.
"You legged it all these miles? Didn't they tell you it's so far
to my place that crows pack a lunch before setting out?
If you're hungry, you'll find bread and sidemeat in the kitchen."
"Thanks."
"And open a can of peaches while you're at it."
Lonesome John resumed the checker game, though his mind
was no longer on it.

The hired hand finished his meal. "I'll chop you some
stove wood before I head back."
"Just a stick or two will be fine."
Lonesome John finished up the checker game, but felt
foolish with a stranger looking on. He was careful not to
talk aloud to the scarecrow, but he thought, "Seems like
a nice enough lad, don't he, Scarebird?"

When he returned to the back porch, the hired hand
was using a whetstone on the blade.
"The axe needs sharpening."
Lonesome John grinned a little. "It usually does.
Wouldn't mind some help with the weeds, if you'd
care to stay a day or so."
"Glad to. My name's Sam."
"There's a room off the barn. You can sleep there."

After supper Lonesome John sat on the porch, but he didn't play his nickle-plated harmonica. He'd feel uncomfortable with a stranger about the place. He gazed off at the scarecrow standing lonely under the darkening sky.

"See you tomorrow, Scarebird," he muttered softly.

Sam spent the morning with the hoe, working away
steady as a clock.
"He's raising blisters on his hands," Lonesome John said
to himself, and pulled the work gloves off the scarecrow.

"Put these on."
"Much obliged, sir."
"My name's John. John Humbuckle."

It took more than a day or so to catch up with the weeds.
The hired hand stayed on, working under the hot sun
without a hat on his head.

"Scarebird," said Lonesome John, "you won't mind if that
young feller borrows your hat."

"Thank you kindly," said the hired hand.

"You from someplace?"

"Used to be."

"Where are your folks?"

"We graved and prayed 'em when I was a little kid."

When the weeding was done, Sam hung up the hoe and pulled off the gloves and hat. "I'll head back."

Lonesome John scratched his neck. "I've been meaning to clear that thornbush in the orchard, if you'd care to stay on a day or so."

"Sure thing."

"Them thorns are meaner'n fishhooks. You'd better wear shoes."

It was raining at first light. Lonesome John pulled the shoes
off the scarecrow, then the yellow slicker.
"The boy'll be ever so grateful, Scarebird."
It was almost a week before they had the last of the
thornbush grubbed out and burned.

After supper, the hired hand joined Lonesome John on
the porch. "I never saw a scarecrow with yellow-painted
eyes. I had a dog once with yellow eyes. He was a mighty
good friend. I'll never forget him."
"That's the way it is with good friends."

"Job's done. Time for me to clear out tomorrow."
And then Sam pulled a harmonica out of his pocket
and began to play a joyful tune.
Lonesome John was silent for a long time, listening.
Then he said, "It's time to start harvesting the crops,
if you want to stay on a day or so, or a week or so."
"Yes, sir. Sure thing."

Lonesome John had been fingering the harmonica in his own
hip pocket like an itch that needed scratching. Now he
pulled it out and smiled broadly. "Do you know this tune?"
He began to play, working his right hand like a bird's wing to
polish up the notes. When he was finished, Sam tapped
his harmonica. "Do you know this one?"

They played, one after another, until full dark. When it was time to turn in, John Humbuckle looked over at the scarecrow for a long moment and then turned to Sam. "Do you play checkers?"